For Maureen and John

First published 2011 by Macmillan Children's Books. This edition published 2018 by
Two Hoots, an imprint of Pan Macmillan,
20 New Wharf Road, London N1 9RR. Associated companies throughout the world.

ISBN 978-1-5098-8472-8

A CIP catalogue record for this book is available from the British Library.

The illustrations in this book were created using pencil and watercolour.

www.twohootsbooks.com
www.emilygravett.com
Printed in China

ROLL UP! ROLL UP! ROLL UP! ROLL UP!

I can stand him on a stool!

I can dress him in a bow...

I can ride him like a horse but WOLF WON'T BITE!

I can make him jump

through hoops!

I can lift him off the ground!

I can make him dance a jig but...

WOLF
WON'T
BITE!

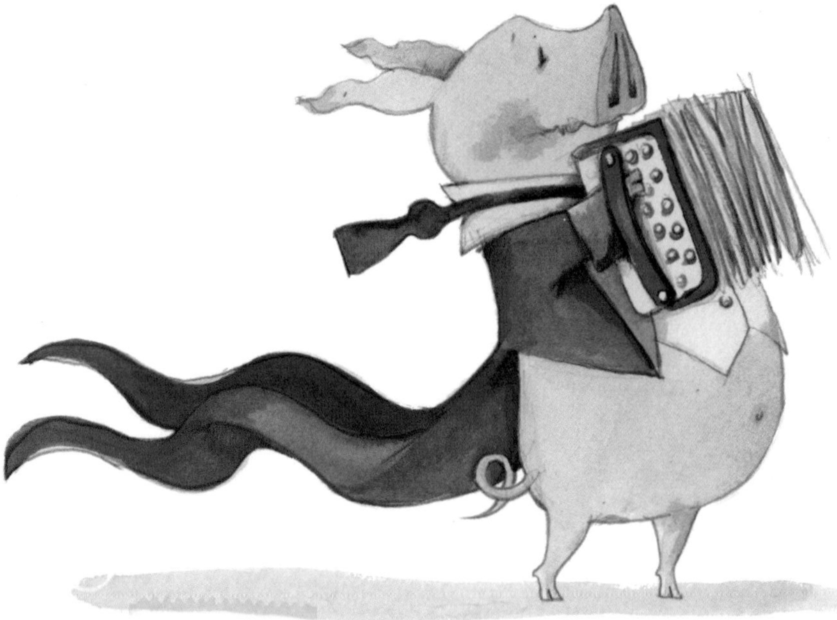

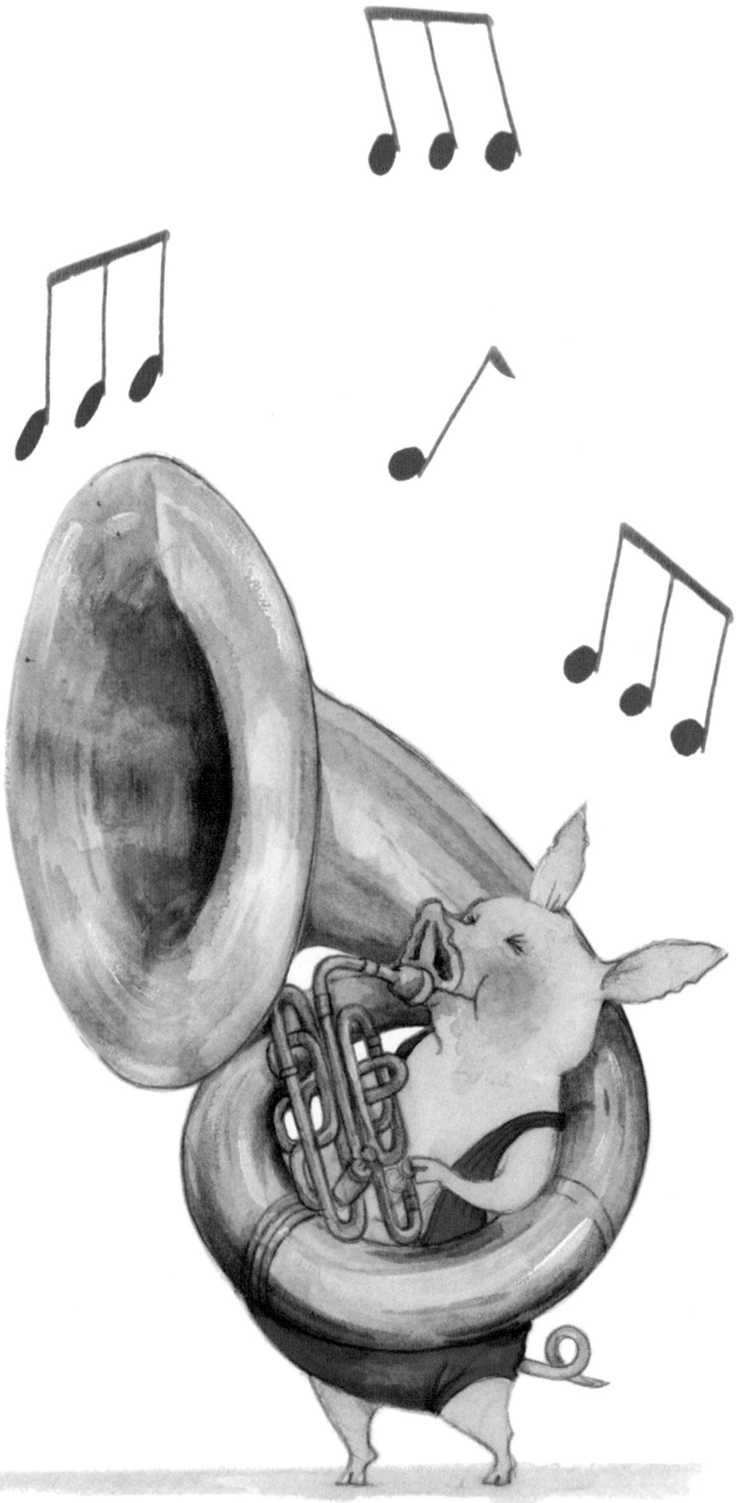

I can miss him EVERY time!

I can shoot him

through the air!

WOLF WON'T BITE!

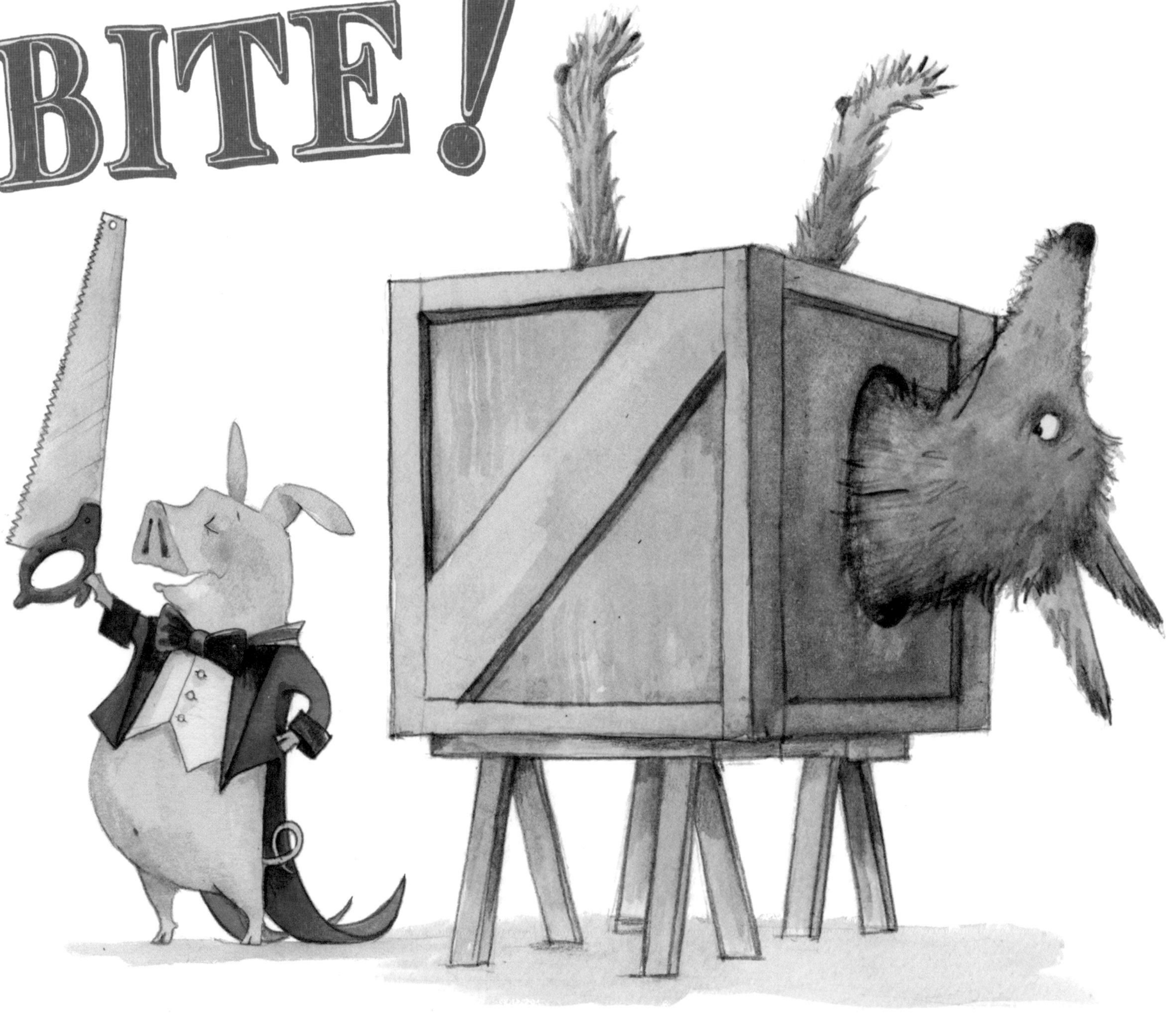

We can even place our heads between his mighty jaws

but
WOLF
WON'T...